In Memory of Michael Murphy
– M.C.

For Mum & Dad
– G.W.

Reprinted 1996

Published in 1994 by Magi Publications
22 Manchester Street, London W1M 5PG

Text © 1994 Michael Coleman
Illustrations © 1994 Gwyneth Williamson

The right of Michael Coleman to be identified as the author
of this work has been asserted by him in accordance with
The Copyright, Designs and Patents Act 1988.

Printed and bound in Italy
by Grafiche AZ, Verona

ISBN 1 85430 262 0

LAZY OZZIE

by

Michael Coleman

illustrated by

Gwyneth Williamson

Magi Publications, London

Ozzie was a very lazy owl.

"It's time you tried
to fly," said Mother
Owl one day.
But Ozzie just said,
"Oh, do I have to?"
Ozzie didn't fancy flying one little bit. It seemed
much too much hard work, all that wing-flapping.
He just wanted to sit around all day.
"I'm practising being wise," he said.

"Well, I want you to fly,'
said Mother Owl sternly.
"Now I'm going off to look
for some food. And if you *are* wise,
you will be on the ground by the time I come back!'

Ozzie thought hard.

If he was wise, then he should be able to think of a way of getting down to the ground without flying.

Suddenly he noticed the horse who lived in their barn. The horse's head came up almost as high as the beam Ozzie was sitting on.

Ozzie had an idea . . .

"Help, help," he yelled.
"What's the matter with you, then?"
said the high horse.

"It's an emergency!" shouted Ozzie, jumping on
to the high horse's back. "Take me to the
cowshed!"

So the high horse
took Ozzie to the cowshed.

In the cowshed there lived a cow who wasn't
quite as high as the high horse.
"It's an emergency!" cried Ozzie, jumping on
to the not-quite-so-high cow's back.
"Take me to the pigsty!"

So the high horse and the not-quite-so-high cow took Ozzie to the pigsty.

In the pigsty there lived a big pig.
"It's an emergency!" cried Ozzie, jumping on to
the big pig's back. "Take me to the farmyard!"

So the high horse,
    the not-quite-so-high cow
    and the big pig took Ozzie
    to the farmyard.

In the farmyard there lived a sheepdog.
The sheepdog wasn't as tall as the
big pig. He was a short sheepdog.
"It's an emergency!" cried Ozzie, jumping
on to the short sheepdog's back.
"Take me to the big field!"

So the high horse, the not-quite-so-high cow, the big pig and the short sheepdog took Ozzie to the big field.

In the big field there lived a little lamb.
"It's an emergency!" cried Ozzie, jumping
on to the little lamb's back. "Take me
to the duck-pond!"

So the high horse, the not-quite-so-high cow, the big pig, the short sheepdog and the little lamb took Ozzie to the duck-pond.

In the duck-pond there lived a diddy duck.
"It's an emergency!" cried Ozzie, jumping on
to the diddy duck's back. "Take me to the barn!"

So the high horse, the not-quite-so-high cow,
the big pig, the short sheepdog,
the little lamb and the diddy duck
took Ozzie back to the barn...

As soon as they got there, Ozzie hopped from the
diddy duck's back down to the ground.
He'd done it!
Now that's what you call being wise,
he told himself!

"So where's the emergency?" asked the high horse.
"Ah," said Ozzie. "I was only joking. What a hoot, eh?"

The high horse, the not-quite-so-high cow, the big pig,
the short sheepdog, the little lamb and the diddy
duck weren't amused.
They all went away grumbling.
But Ozzie was pleased. His plan had worked.
He was pretty wise already.

"I flew all the way down,"
he said to Mother Owl when
she came back.

Mother Owl gave a big smile.
"Well done, son," she said.
Ozzie thought she was
pleased with him . . .

. . . but he didn't know she'd been watching all the time. "Now let me see you fly back up again," said Mother Owl.